Starbright Nights

written
and
illustrated by

Carlos Maggette

For Ernestine Maggette, who believed
that I'd actually finish this book.
Now thats some kinda' imagination.

Before bedtime my bedroom glows.
The moon and stars shine through my
window.

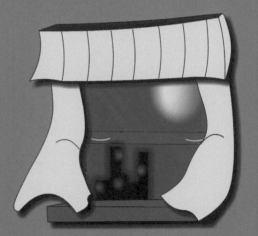

I often wish to be among the stars
as they dazzle, twinkle and glow all
around me.

Just like an astronaut, I want to travel beyond Earth's atmosphere and enter Outer space.

And then I close my eyes, fall asleep, and I DREAM.

Magically, my bed transforms into a SPACESHIP ready for take- off!

Up and away I go soaring through the night sky.
I fly my spaceship swiftly towards the stars.

Upon reaching Outer space I encounter other space explorers traveling the galaxy just like me.

I also see many different planets and stars.
Some are VERY strange and unusual!

I approach a WORMHOLE in space
on a planet known as The Apple Core.

Not surprisingly, the beings who live there
all have very bright smiles.

I also observe a star wearing shades. Wow!
It looks so cool! It must be a MOVIE STAR!

Next I encounter the legendary alien known as ZoomZoom Van Vroom!

ZoomZoom Van Vroom is the fastest spaceship racer in the ENTIRE galaxy!

Finish

Start

ZoomZoom challenges me to a race around
a racetrack known as The Whrling Vortex.

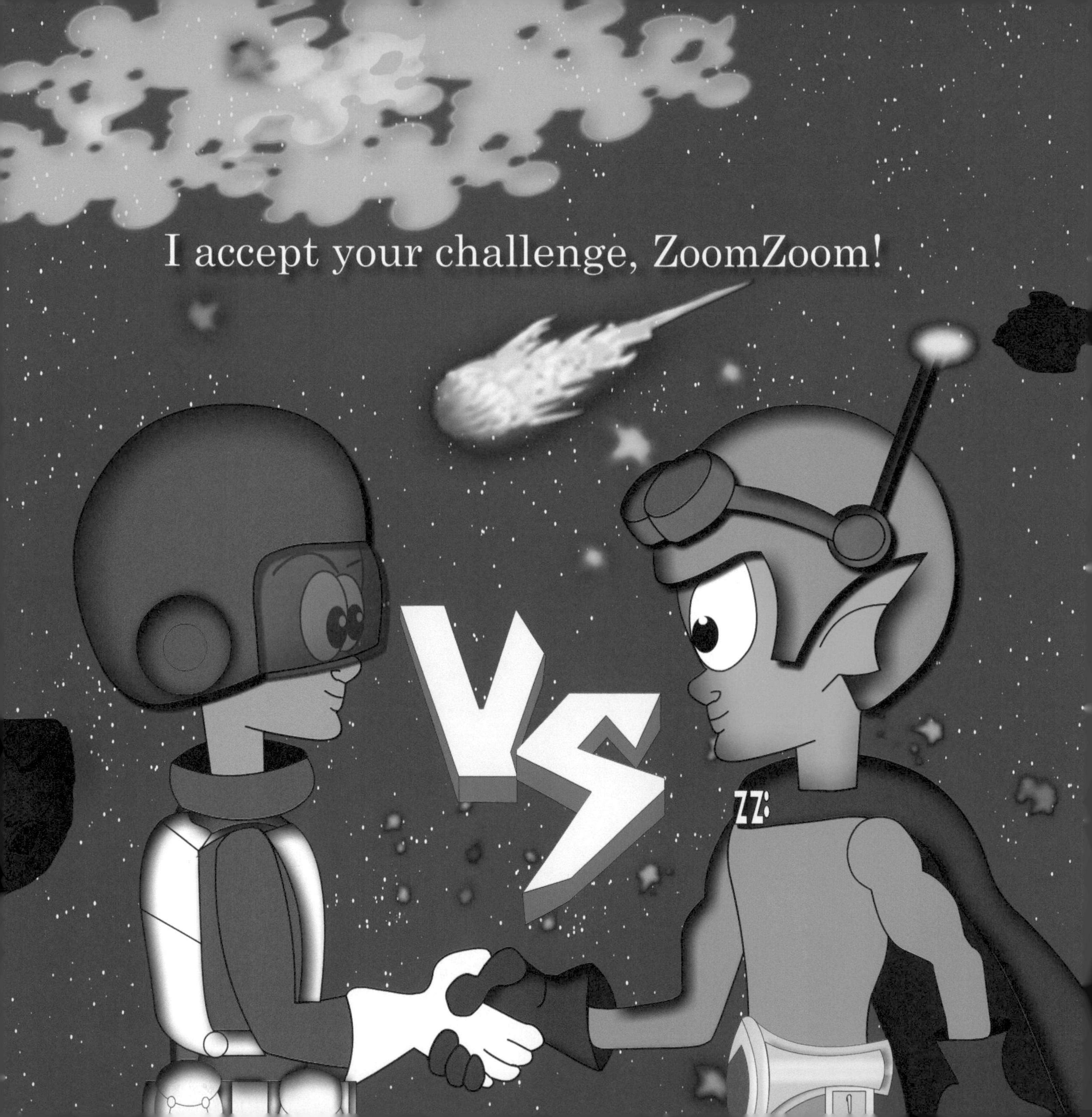
I accept your challenge, ZoomZoom!
VS
ZZ

We start our engines at the starting line.
The light turns green and away we go!

ZoomZoom takes the lead. Oh, man!
This could be trouble. I must think fast!

I'll try using a TURBO BOOST to gain extra speed. I sure hope this works!

Great, it worked! I have taken the lead!
See you later rather than soon,
ZoomZoom Van Vroom!

YES! I win! It was a very close race though. I am happy to have won against such a great competitor.

ZoomZoom Van Vroom congratulates me. He is not only a great racer, he is also a good sport as well. Thanks, ZoomZoom!

Now its time for me to return home to Earth.
I must hurry because I have school in the morning.

The End

CPSIA information can be obtained
at www.ICGtesting.com
Printed in the USA
LVHW071928151118
597258LV00011B/110/P

* 9 7 8 0 6 1 5 9 9 9 6 4 7 *